Pooh's E
Egg Hunt

Disney's
Winnie the Pooh First Readers

A Winnie the Pooh First Reader

Pooh's Easter Egg Hunt

by Isabel Gaines

ILLUSTRATED BY Studio Orlando

NEW YORK

Pooh's Easter Egg Hunt

"Happy Easter!" Winnie the Pooh
called to his friends.

They were all at Rabbit's house

for his Easter egg hunt.

"All right, everybody," Rabbit said.

"Whoever finds the most eggs wins.

Get ready . . . get set . . . go!"

Pooh, Piglet, Roo, Tigger,

Eeyore, and Kanga

ran into the woods.

Pooh found a yellow egg

under some daffodils.

He put the egg in his basket.

Poor Pooh didn't know

his basket

had a hole in it.

The yellow egg slipped out

and fell onto the soft grass.

Piglet found the yellow egg.

"Lucky me!" he said.

Then Pooh found a purple egg

behind a rock.

He put the purple egg

in his basket.

Oops! This egg slipped out, too.

13

Roo found the purple egg.

"Oh, goody!" he cried.

"Purple's my favorite color!"

Pooh found a green egg in a tree,

and put it in his basket.

He didn't see it fall back out.

Tigger found the green egg.

"Hoo-hoo-hoo!" Tigger cried.

"I'm on my way to winning!"

Next Pooh found a red egg . . .

that slipped through the hole

and into a clump of thistle.

Eeyore found the red egg.

"Surprise," he mumbled.

"I found an Easter egg."

On the side of a grassy hill,

Pooh found a blue egg.

"How pretty."

Pooh continued up the hill—

as the egg rolled down it.

Kanga found Pooh's blue egg

lodged against a log.

Finally, Rabbit shouted, "Time's up!"

Everyone gathered around.

"Let's see who won," Rabbit said.

Piglet, Roo, Tigger, Eeyore,

and Kanga showed their Easter eggs.

Pooh looked inside his empty basket. "My eggs seem to be hiding again," he said.

Piglet looked at Pooh's basket.

"I think I know where," Piglet said,

poking his hand through the hole.

"You can have my yellow egg,"
said Piglet. "It was probably
your egg before it was mine."

"Thank you, Piglet," said Pooh.

"You can have my purple egg,

too," said Roo.

"Here, Buddy Bear," said Tigger.
"Tiggers only like to win
fair and square."

"Too good to be true," muttered Eeyore, giving Pooh his red egg.

"And here's my blue egg," Kanga said.

29

"You're the winner, Pooh!"

Rabbit said.

"You win an Easter feast."

"Is there enough food

for my friends

to eat, too?" Pooh asked.

"I could make more,"

Rabbit said.

"Is there enough honey?" asked Pooh.

"There's plenty of honey," said Rabbit.

"Then let's eat!" said Pooh.

33

Everyone had a wonderful time.

Pooh enjoyed the food—

especially the honey!

Can you match the words with the pictures?

Kanga

basket

daffodil

purple

green

36

Fill in the missing letters.

P_oh

h_le

re_

_og

_oo

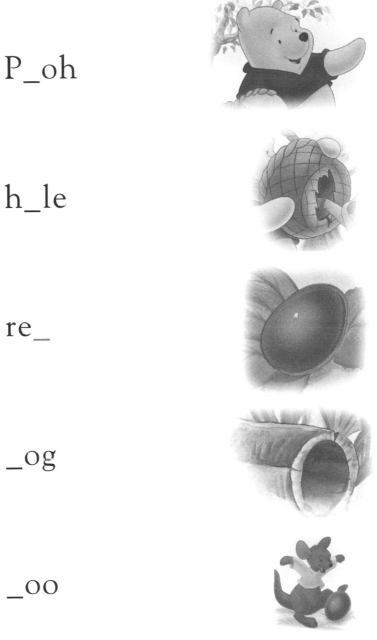

Join the Pooh Friendship Club!

A wonder-filled year of friendly
activities and interactive fun for your child!

The fun starts with:

- Clubhouse play kit
- Exclusive club T-shirt
- The first issue of "Pooh News"
- Toys, stickers and gifts
  from Pooh

The fun goes on with:

- Quarterly issues of "Pooh News" each
  with special surprises
- Birthday and Friendship Day cards
  from Pooh
- And more!

Join now and also get a colorful, collectible Pooh art print

Yearly membership costs just $25
plus 15 Hunny Pot Points.
(Look for Hunny Pot Points 3
on Pooh products.)

To join, send check or money order and
Hunny Pot Points to:

Pooh Friendship Club
P.O. Box 1723
Minneapolis, MN 55440-1723

Please include the following information:
Parent name, child name, complete address,
phone number, sex (M/F), child's birthday,
and child's T-shirt size (S, M, L)
(CA and MN residents add applicable sales tax.)

Call toll-free for more information
1-888-FRNDCLB

Kit materials not intended for children under 3 years of age. Kit
materials subject to change without notice. Please allow 8-10 weeks for
delivery. Offer expires 6/30/99. Offer good while supplies last. Please do
not send cash. Void where restricted or prohibited by law. Quantities may
be limited. Disney is not liable for correspondence, requests, or orders
delayed, illegible, lost or stolen in the mail. Offer valid in the U.S. and
Canada only. ©Disney. Based on the "Winnie the Pooh" works, copyright
A.A. Milne and E.H. Shepard.

Fun
for kids
ages 3-8!

Pooh
Friendship
Club

Pooh

21

Wonderfully Whimsical Ways To Bring Winnie The Pooh Into Your Child's Life.

Pooh FRIENDSHIP

Pooh and the gang help children learn about liking each other for who they are in 5 charming volumes about what it means to be a friend.

Pooh STORYBOOK CLASSICS

These 4 enchanting volumes let you share the original A.A. Milne stories – first shown in theaters – you so fondly remember from your own childhood.

Pooh PLAYTIME

Children can't help but play and pretend with Pooh and his friends in 5 playful volumes that celebrate the joys of being young.

Pooh LEARNING

Pooh and his pals help children discover sharing and caring in 5 loving volumes about growing up.

FREE*
Flash Cards Attached!
A Different Set With Each *Pooh Learning* Video!
* With purchase, while supplies last.